Published in Canada and the USA in 2020
by Groundwood Books

Groundwood Books / House of Anansi Press
groundwoodbooks.com

We gratefully acknowledge the Government of Canada for its financial support of our publishing program.

With the participation of the Government of Canada
Avec la participation du gouvernement du Canada | Canadä

Library and Archives Canada Cataloguing in Publication
Title: Cave paintings / Jairo Buitrago ; pictures by Rafael Yockteng ; translated by Elisa Amado.
Other titles: Pinturas rupestres. English
Names: Buitrago, Jairo, author. | Yockteng, Rafael, illustrator. | Amado, Elisa, translator.
Description: Translation of: Las pinturas rupestres.
Identifiers: Canadiana (print) 20190223898 | Canadiana (ebook) 20190224495 | ISBN 9781773061726 (hardcover) | ISBN 9781773061733 (EPUB) | ISBN 9781773064222 (Kindle)
Classification: LCC PZ7.B8857 Cav 2020 | DDC j863/.7—dc23

The illustrations were done digitally.
Design by Michael Solomon
Printed and bound in China

For the unknown stars in difficult neighborhoods.
— RY

CAVE PAINTINGS

JAIRO BUITRAGO
PICTURES BY RAFAEL YOCKTENG
TRANSLATED BY ELISA AMADO

GROUNDWOOD BOOKS
HOUSE OF ANANSI PRESS
TORONTO BERKELEY

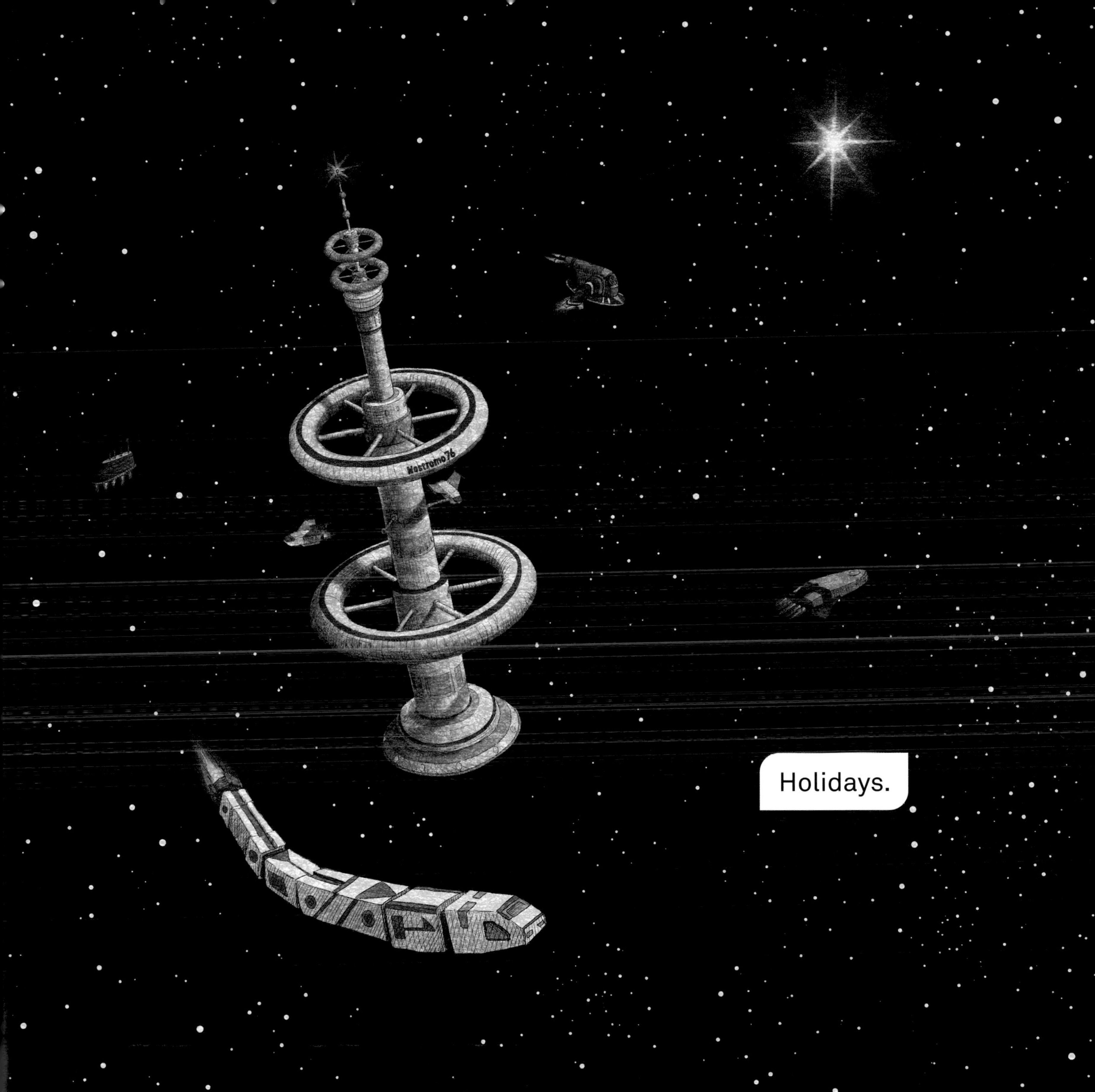
Nostromo76
Holidays.

I can't wait to go see
my grandmother.

Just like me, everyone is
anxious to take off . . .

Nostromo76

. . . to the stars.

I have a note for the flight attendant. So I won't get lost.

But I don't really need it, I think, because I've seen all of this so many times.

Always traveling alone.

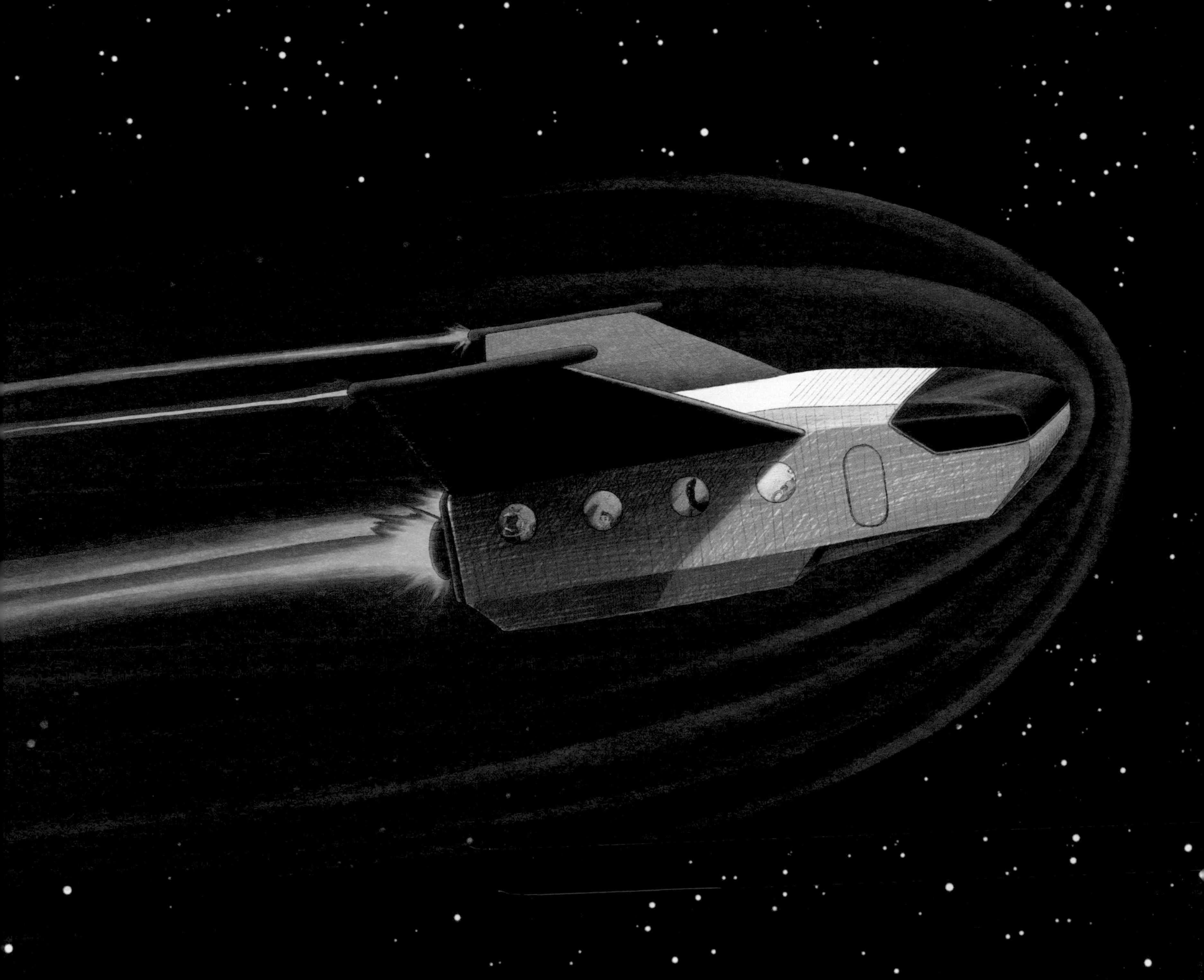

Sometimes they ask me, "Why are you always going to the farthest planet?"

Traveling alone like a comet

to a dim,
distant star
in the Big Dipper.

Because it’s worth it

to cross one universe

to explore another.

to see a man's hand

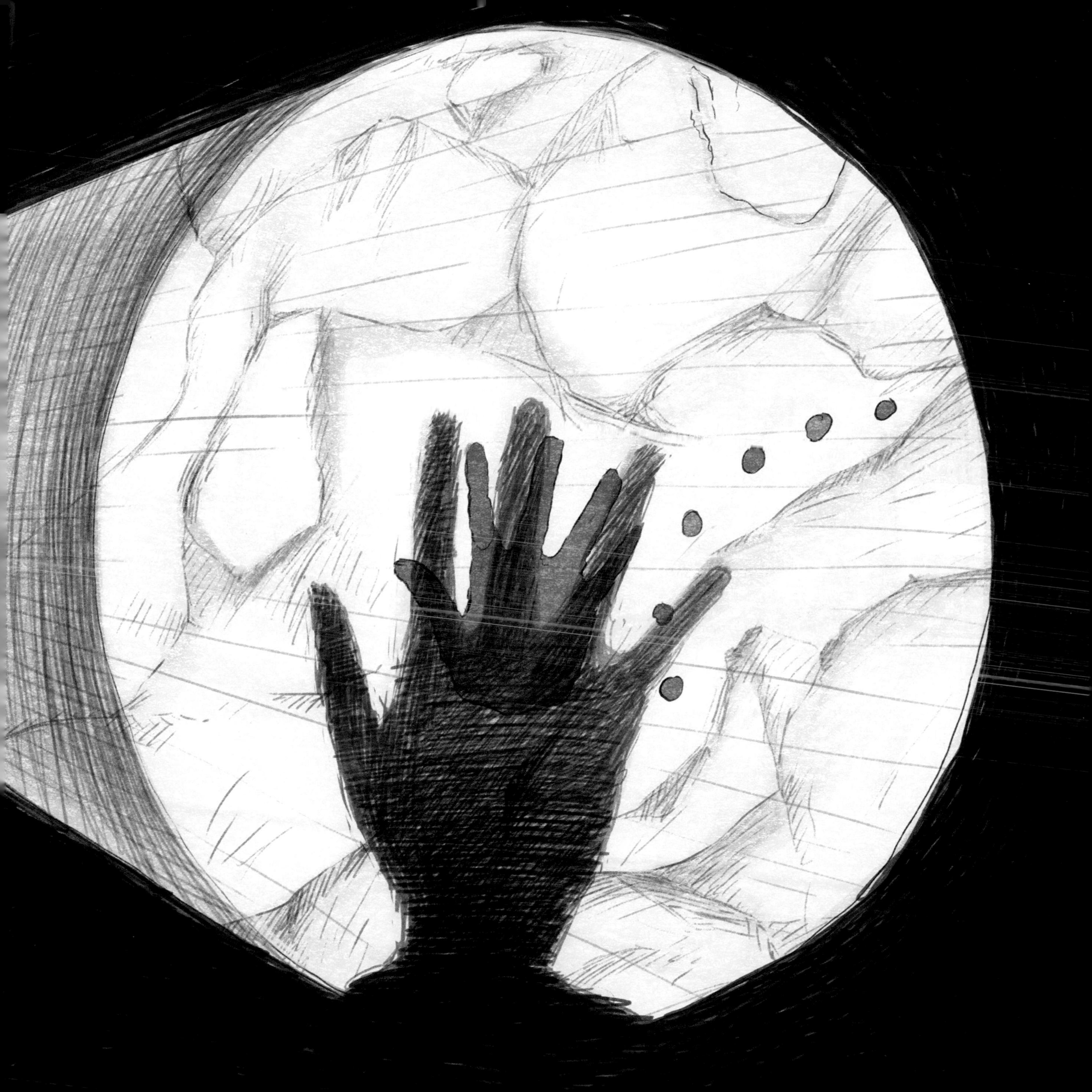

next to so many animals.

When I got home, I was so tired I couldn't sleep.

They were good for making marks on paper. She gave me that too.

And I used them on the way home

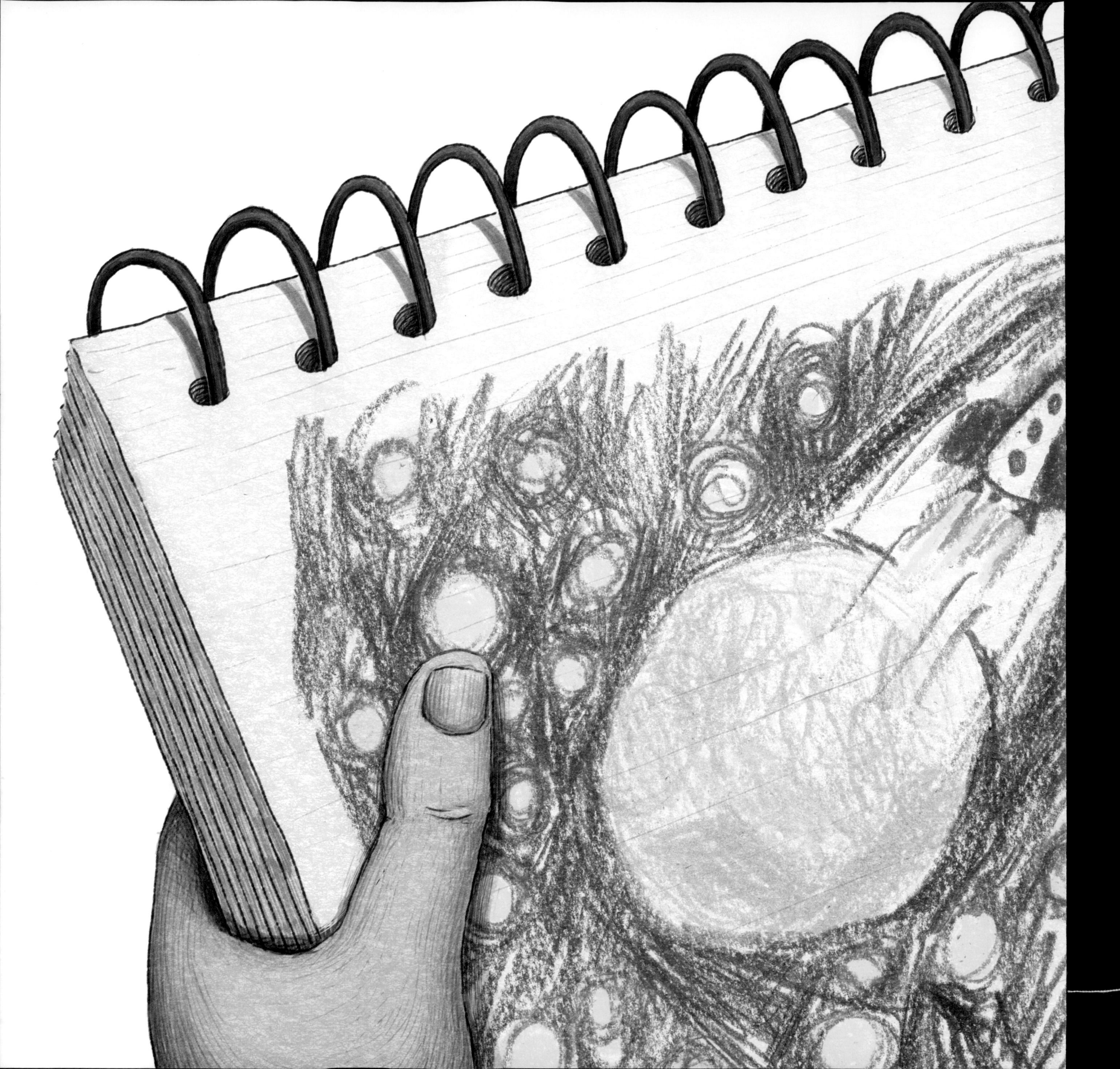

to draw what I could see out the window.

Because what I could see was infinity.